A Nature Survival Guide

WHAT TO DO IF YOU MEET A BEAR?

Štěpánka Sekaninová • Adam Wolf

ALBATROS

CONTENTS

INTRODUCTION

Is there any better way to relax than going on a walk deep in the woods? The lovely smells of nature, the rustling of trees, the babbling of brooks, the cracking of pine needles underfoot . . . If we have a sweet tooth, our parents can help us pick strawberries, blueberries, raspberries, blackberries, or huckleberries, depending on the time of year.

If we get tired and need to rest, there is no softer bed than one made of grass. Are the woods not the perfect place to relax?

This walk is bound to clear your head of heavy thoughts. You will go home with a happy heart.

It could happen, however, that you lose your way on a mysterious woodland path. It could even happen that you meet an enraged wild boar – deep in the woods or out in the open.

Don't be discouraged from going on country and woodland walks, though. You don't need to be at home to stay safe. This book will give you simple, fun instructions on what to do if you should get lost outdoors or happen to find yourself face to face with a dangerous animal. Let's go through these together so that you can stay safe and have fun.

WHAT TO DO IF YOU ARE LOST IN THE WOODS

You have just gotten lost in the wilderness. You call out at the top of your lungs, but no one hears you. Don't worry, though. There are things you can do to help yourself.

POINT 1

The first thing to do is sit down and calmly think through your circumstances. A person who gives in to stress and confusion is likely to make mistakes. If the fog is thick, stay where you are until it clears. Where the light is bad, you could step into a pothole and sprain your ankle, or – heaven forbid! – fall from a cliff.

Once the fog clears, get your bearings. If you get thirsty, drink whatever water you have on you.

POINT 2

Have you found a stream or a spring for water? You have? Great! Even so, never drink unfiltered liquid. First either boil it (A) or carry it around all day in a plastic bottle tied to your backpack (B) – UV rays will filter it pretty well.

Just make sure to build a fire and boil the moss water before drinking it. The bacteria in moss can make you sick unless you boil it away.

Moss is full of water.

You can collect dew by tying a piece of clothing around your foot or lower leg and walking through tall dewy grass. The clothing will soak in the moisture for you to then wring out. This may not be the best thing you have ever drunk, but don't forget that you are fighting for survival.

Collecting dew

POINT 3

Water problem solved! But there's still no sign of rescuers. It seems you have no choice but to spend the night in the wilderness. As evening falls, you begin to feel cold. You must warm yourself up. You need a fire! If you happen to have a fire striker, you're all set. If you don't, find two pieces of quartz and rub them together.

Don't worry if you can't find quartz. You can also start a fire by rubbing a stick against another piece of wood. But both rubbing methods are incredibly hard and demand a great deal of patience. Still, you must persevere!

Kindling (dry grass) C	Kindling (dry twigs)	Put the stick in the hole to turn the log . .

stick	log with hole	
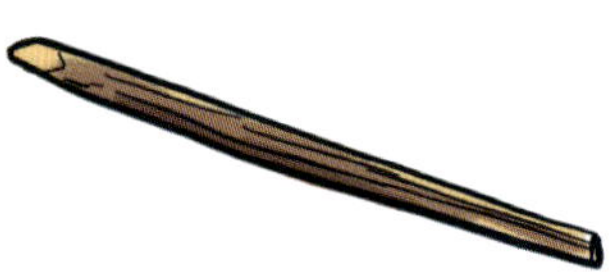		

Brilliant! Your fire is contained within a ring of stones, so that it doesn't set the forest alight. Now you must build a primitive shelter to spend the night in.

Always surround your fire with stones to prevent it from spreading.

As soon as smoke appears, add the kindling.

Kindling can also be lit by rubbing two pieces of quartz together.

Without tinder (C) made of dry plants or twigs, you won't get a fire started. But where will you find it in wet conditions? Look for a secluded place – under an overhanging rock, for instance.

POINT 4

Improvised shelters such as caves, rock overhangs, haystacks, and hunting blinds require no work on your part. But if no such shelter is in view, you'll need to make a shelter out of tree branches. If you do find a cave, beware! It may be home to an animal that doesn't wish to share it with you!

Don't build your shelter where water may collect.

You may be surprised to learn that snow is a great insulator. People who live in frozen places build their shelters – igloos – with it.

The top of a hill is exposed to possible wind and lightning.

Are there many old or dead trees around? One might fall on your shelter . . .

Find two trees and wedge a long leafy branch between them. Lean other large branches against this before adding more leaves for warmth and insulation. If you can find enough of the right kind of branch, get lots of them and make them into a big pile for a comfortable bed.

Do you need to spend the night in a snowy place? Well, just use the snow that's around you! A layer of snow over the branches of your shelter will keep it warm enough. If there is a lot of snow, you can make your whole shelter out of it!

WHAT TO DO IF YOU ARE LOST IN THE DESERT

Claw your way up the nearest dune and throw sand in the air, as a signal to anyone nearby that you are lost. Walk in the early morning or evening, when it is coolest; otherwise, rest up. If you have food or water, eat or drink it whenever you'd like – trusting that you'll find more later, when you need it. Explore the desert valley, where you are most likely to find water.

Yay! You've found water! Now you can eat something. Cactus fruit liquid is delicious to drink. Lizards, too, are quite tasty to eat, and there are more than enough of them out in the desert.

CACTI ARE GREAT LIQUID CONTAINERS. CUT INTO THEIR FLESHY LEAVES AND YOUR THIRST WILL BE QUENCHED.

WHAT TO DO IF YOU ARE LOST IN THE JUNGLE

Animal tracks will lead you to water. If you find a large body of water, stay close to it. The crew of a plane is more likely to spot you there than in dense jungle.

Be careful where you tread. The jungle is crawling with all kinds of venomous snakes, beetles, spiders, and other hard-to-spot but super dangerous creatures.

Don't eat everything you find. A lot of plants in the jungle are poisonous. And if you have no choice but to sleep in the jungle, don't lie on uncovered ground. Make a bed of palm leaves, thus reducing your contact with unwanted creepy-crawlies.

WHAT TO DO IF YOU MEET A BEAR

Uh-oh – a bear. But they haven't noticed you. Leave as quietly as you can, watching the bear from the corner of your eye to check what they're doing.

People try to avoid encounters with bears. And bears are keen to avoid people: they may have the strength of ten men, sharp claws and teeth, but still they are afraid of us. Unfortunately, when they do meet us, they feel threatened, and so tend to defend themselves. Therefore, it is necessary to be cautious around a bear and convince them that we mean them no harm.

Oh dear. A bear has noticed you! Whatever you do, don't look them in the eye – they will take this as an invitation to attack. Retreat slowly, ideally sideways. Do not lose sight of the bear. Do not make any sudden movements, least of all a mad dash for it!

Whatever you do, don't try to scare the bear away!

The bear has stood up on their hind legs. Keep a cool head, though. When a bear stands, they are just trying to get a better sense of things, that's all . . . They find their way around mainly by smell.

Oh no! The bear is about to attack. Kneel down and curl into a ball. If they are a grizzly, this is the only way to divert their attention. If they are a black bear, try intimidation: wave your arms, shout, clap, and bang on whatever is handy.

WHAT TO DO IF YOU MEET A WILD BOAR

The wild boar is an extremely shy animal. Their excellent sense of smell and hearing usually enable them to pick up on unwelcome guests and flee the scene before they're noticed. Sometimes, though, they overlook a visitor to their territory – and a meeting occurs. What happens next?

!

IF YOU MEET A WILD BOAR, DO NOT LOOK THEM IN THE EYE. TRY TO LEAVE THEIR TERRITORY CALMLY, KEEPING YOUR MOVEMENTS TO A MINIMUM. THIS USUALLY WORKS.

bristled fur, grunting

gnashing teeth

If there is a tree or a haystack nearby, climb up it. As a wild boar is a speedy creature – they can run up to 30 miles per hour! – it is best to wait in a safe place for their anger to pass.

Uh-oh! The fur on this wild boar's back is bristled. They are grunting, smacking their lips, and gnashing their teeth. They're about to attack! What are you waiting for? Run!
(A boar will run after you for a while but will soon give up.)

WHAT TO DO IF YOU MEET A BULL

A raging bull snorts and rakes the ground with his foot.

The bull is a very dangerous animal, especially when angry. If you happen to cross one's path right then, you will regret it.

Should you find yourself in the presence of a bull, though, DO NOT TURN YOUR BACK on him, no matter what. If a switch goes off inside his head, he will attack before you know what is happening!

The bull will stand at an angle to you with his neck bent, telling you to get out of his way if you know what's good for you. It is hard not to panic, but you must move out of the bull's eyeline calmly and make no sudden movements.

But you are still in the bull's eyeline. He are now facing you with his head down and shoulders hunched, and he is scraping the ground with his hooves, sending soil flying. You are in very great danger. You need to get out of sight as soon as possible.

That bulls are provoked by the sight of red is a myth. Your chances with the bull if you are wearing red are the same as with any other color.

NEVER RUN FROM A BULL: YOU WON'T STAND A CHANCE! SIMPLY DO ALL YOU CAN TO AVOID MEETING ONE IN THE FIRST PLACE.

WHAT TO DO IF YOU MEET A DOG

Dogs may be our best-loved and most loyal friends, but an aggressive dog on the loose can be as dangerous as a bear. So, what should you do if such an animal confronts you?

HOW TO TELL IF A DOG MEANS TO ATTACK YOU

Don't look them in the eye. Don't run away. Stand still with your arms crossed over your chest. If there is a stick within reach, pick it up. Stay calm, even if you are up against a pack of dogs. You shouldn't let a dog smell your fear.

They fix their gaze on you.

Their fur bristles.

They bare their teeth.

They growl menacingly.

Uh-oh, a shepherd dog . . .
Also a problem!

You are walking through a meadow where curly-coated sheep are grazing on the grass. It's lovely. But there is a dog whose job it is to protect the herd with his life. He sees you as his sheep's enemy. What ever will you do?

If the herd is spread across the meadow, you have no choice but to pass through their pasture. Walk calmly, hoping the shepherd dog will accompany you the whole way without attacking.

WHAT TO DO?

1) Keep calm.
2) Make no sudden movements.
3) If you are on a bike, get off it. Try to retreat from the herd's territory as you pass through the meadow.
4) Once the dog stops barking menacingly and does nothing more than watch you, you are in the clear. Congratulations!

The same advice applies for all canines. Should you encounter a coyote, for instance, don't run away: they would catch up with you in a flash. To scare away a coyote, shout, stomp your feet, and throw whatever you can grab. As with all predatory animals, never turn your back on them.

WHAT TO DO IF YOU MEET A SNAKE

Snakes do not wish for contact with humans. The slightest noise will send them slithering away. Even so, one may cross your path. If it does, simply change direction and go the other way.

Snakes never attack just for fun. They do so only when they feel threatened. Never stick your hands into a hole or a crevice in a rock without checking first. It might just be the home of a snake!

If you wish to keep snakes well away, be loud – stomp your feet, clap, whoop . . . This will scare any snakes into fleeing.

WHAT TO DO IF YOU MEET A MONKEY

A monkey may look really cute, but looks can be deceiving. If they don't like something, like you refusing to share your snack, they can get very aggressive and give you a nasty bite.

Beware! Monkeys are mischievous. They're always up to something!

So if you encounter one, stay away, guard your things, and do not look them in the eye.

WHAT TO DO IF YOU MEET A BUCK

A buck (a male deer) is a majestic animal. Although it is not a predator, a blow from its hooves or a poke from its pointed antlers is no joke. So what should you do if you are unlucky enough to cross one's path?

!

NEVER APPROACH FAWNS (BABY DEER) ON THEIR OWN. YOU CAN BE SURE THAT THEIR PARENTS WILL BE NEARBY, FULLY PREPARED TO FIGHT FOR THEIR OFFSPRING.

Believe it or not, bucks are timid. Given the choice, they will run away from you. But if they feel that you are a threat to them or – heaven forbid! – their young, look out!

To protect yourself, you can hide behind something big.

On encountering a stag, retreat slowly and keep changing direction. This strategy will confuse them.

If there's nowhere to hide, try to look bigger than the stag.

Raise your hands above your head and wave your jacket. Make yourself appear bigger than you actually are to the buck. If nothing else can be done, climb a tree.

WHAT TO DO IF YOU MEET AN ELK

Elk are not aggressive predators, but it is best to keep your distance from them and their mighty antlers. If the elk you encounter is hungry, scared, or out of sorts, they may be a threat.

When an elk pins back their ears, bristles the fur on their neck, licks themself, and growls, it is no time to play the hero.

An elk can be over six feet tall!

As with a buck, make sure that there is some kind of obstacle between you and an elk – specifically its hooves. If you happen to fall as you run, curl up and protect your head. Stay this way until the elk goes away. Otherwise, it might attack again.

As a last resort, just curl up into a ball.

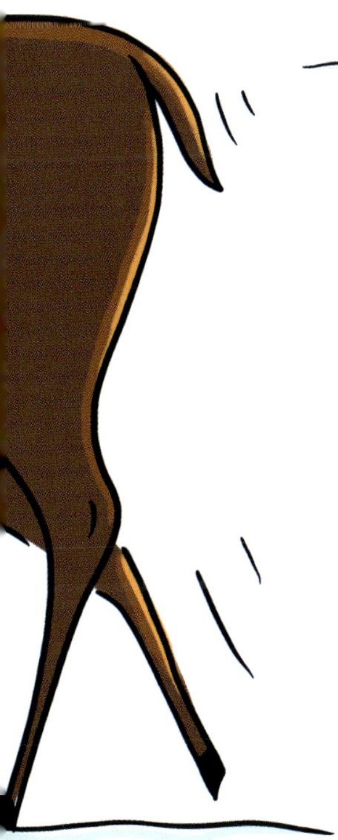

An elk licking itself, with its ears pinned back and its neck fur bristling, is preparing to attack. Gather your strength and run away! It won't take the elk long to catch you!

WHAT TO DO IF YOU MEET A SHARK

An encounter with this much-feared predator, a menace of the seas, is anything but pleasant! Never enter the ocean where sharks are likely to be swimming around.

Don't wear glittery swimwear or bold jewelry. They will shine in the water, and the shark might mistake you for a tasty, shiny-scaled fish.

Sharks often mistake surfers and divers for seals.

Never enter the water with a bleeding wound. And don't pee in the water. These are both things that can draw a shark's attention.

KEEP AWAY FROM FISHING BOATS, WHERE A SHARK COULD MISTAKE YOU FOR FISH BAIT. COMPLY WITH ALL WARNING SIGNS ON THE BEACH.

Don't swim when it is getting dark – late in the evening or early in the morning. It is best to swim in a group – when sharks attack people, it's usually swimmers who are alone.

YOU HAVE FOLLOWED ALL THE RULES, BUT THE SHARK IS STILL SWIMMING AROUND YOU. WHAT DO YOU DO?

1) Keep calm. Make no sudden movements and try not to splash around.
2) Don't turn your back on the shark. Keep swimming around so that you can keep your eyes on them.
3) Try to swim to the safety of the shore as calmly and quickly as possible.

If you are snorkeling or scuba diving, hide as a fish would hide – behind a reef, where you can observe the shark's behavior.

Don't take your eyes off the shark until you are able to swim away.

OTHER DANGERS AT SEA

The other creatures you meet in the sea will probably be less frightening than sharks. But these, too, can be bothersome.

Jellyfish look innocent enough, but their stinging tentacles can be lethal. If you get stung, bathe the wound with warm (not hot) water until the pain subsides. Then apply a suitable ointment to the wound.

Sea urchins can sting. Simply remove their spines with tweezers and bathe the puncture wounds with warm water.

Have plenty to drink and avoid direct sunlight.

Watch out for rip currents! They're like invisible rivers in the ocean pulling you away from shore. If you get caught in one, stay calm and swim parallel to the beach, not towards it, until you feel the current release you.

WHAT TO DO IF YOU MEET AN ALLIGATOR

If an alligator comes toward you with its big toothy mouth wide open, don't worry! There's something you can do to stay safe.

Your only hope is to try and close the alligator's mouth. This can be done with one hand, as alligators have weak jaw muscles. Even so, it is best to simply avoid such a dangerous encounter in the first place!

For the same reasons, you should avoid swimming in unfamiliar waters.

Walking along a river can be nice. Even so, if you know the river is full of alligators, stay far away. An alligator attacks from the water so sneakily that you won't see it coming.

Fortunately, an alligator soon gets tired, so if you do manage to escape, it won't come after you.

WHAT TO DO IF YOU MEET A TIGER

Very little can help against a tiger attack, so keep far away from places where they are likely to be. But if you happen to meet one . . .

. . . don't look them in the eye, don't turn your back on them, and above all keep calm.

You don't stand much of a chance against them in the water either. They're strong, quick swimmers.

Because tigers are hunted by poachers, they are sadly an endangered species. They may be more afraid of you than you are of them – making them even more dangerous.

WHAT TO DO IF YOU MEET A SCORPION

If the stinger on the scorpion's tail is raised, get out of its way as quickly as possible. This means that it's ready to attack.

The scorpion couldn't care less about you, so wait it out. It will soon lose interest and move on to other things.

A sting from a scorpion is the last thing you need. It is very painful indeed.

NEVER LIE DOWN IN A TENT WITHOUT FIRST CHECKING IT OVER PROPERLY.

Beware of uninvited guests in your tent.

Check your clothes thoroughly – by shaking them out and turning them inside out – before putting them on. A scorpion surprise is a truly unpleasant one!

Don't forget to check your sleeping bag too.

IF YOU GET STUNG BY A SCORPION:

Check your shoes very carefully. If you put on a shoe that a scorpion has made into its bed, you are in for big trouble!

Clean the wound and cool it down. If you find that you cannot swallow, seek medical attention immediately.

WHAT TO DO IF YOU MEET A SWAN

Who could be afraid of the splendid, elegant white swan? Well, this bird is not as fragile as it looks. A swan has the strength of a bull, not least when it is angry – and even more so if it is defending its nest.

Swans should not be approached.

350 feet

100 feet

If you happen to come across an angry swan, don't panic. Raise your hands above your head and wave them around like crazy. Stomp your feet, hiss, and back away slowly. If a stick is within reach, wave it to intimidate the bird more. Stand your ground and do not run away!

KEEPING A SAFE DISTANCE

1) For big game, a safe distance is at least 100 feet – about a quarter the length of a football field.
2) For predatory mammals and other predators, this is at least 400 feet away – the full length of a football field. Keep farther away if you can. If you wish to look at these animals up close, just use binoculars.

TIPS AND TRICKS FOR SURVIVAL IN THE WILD

Congratulations! You have survived to the end of our survival adventure book. In some places, when your life was at stake, you surely broke into a sweat. In others, you probably enjoyed the landscape. Before you go, though, let's repeat some of the most valuable advice.

Now you know that encounters with most wild animals can be avoided by making noise. Many dangerous animals are shy, with no interest in humans or other intruders. So, then, how do we make noises?

by stomping our feet

by clapping

by beating two sticks together

by using our voice

by using a noisemaker for startling bears and wild boars

When you cross paths with an animal, a basic rule is: do not look it in the eye, for it may think eye contact is a call to attack. This applies to people, too. If you see someone who is obviously looking for trouble, do not look them in the eye.

It goes without saying that whenever you're in nature, you need to be properly equipped. This is about more than having the right clothes and shoes. Don't underestimate the value of certain tools and aids: they may save your life. Just make sure to use these under the supervision of an adult!

matches – ideally waterproof ones

flashlight – a source of light

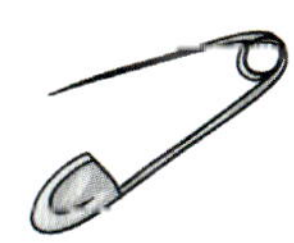

safety pin

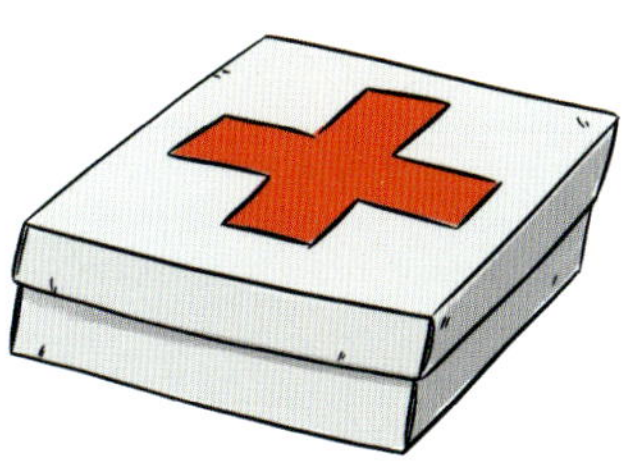

first-aid kit

pocketknife

anti-mosquito spray

5. května 1746/22, Prague 4, Czech Republic
Author: Štěpánka Sekaninová
Illustrations © Adam Wolf, 2024
Translator: Andrew Oakland
Editor: Scott Alexander Jones

Printed in China by Leo Paper Group.

www.albatrosbooks.com

albatros_books_ | Albatros Books | Albatros Books US